P9-DME-305

Richard Burnie

JONATHAN CAPE
LONDON

FOR JACOBA JOHANNA CHRISTINA.

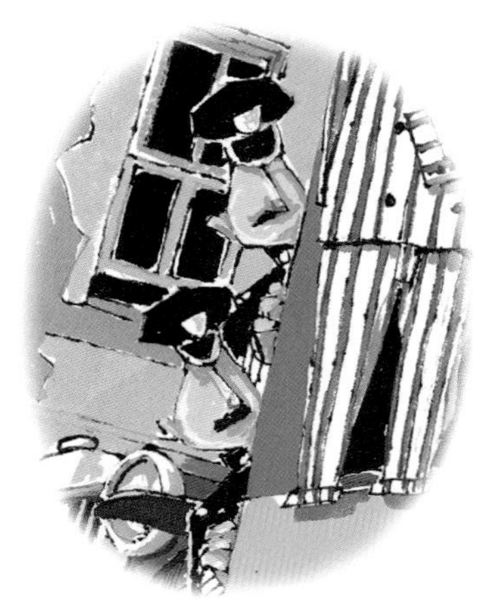

Also by Richard Burnie

MASTERPATH

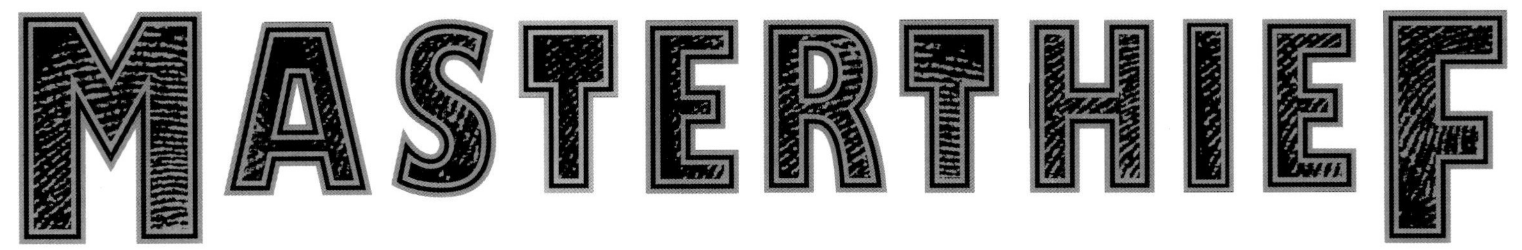

For weeks the city police department have tried unsuccessfully to arrest the mysterious Masterthief responsible for a series of bizarre robberies.

Today, at last, they have an important lead linking Mr Fabrizzi, the owner of a second-hand goods store, to the crimes. Whenever the store runs out of stock, things start disappearing all over the city.

Mr Fabrizzi is clever. He has an uncanny ability to avoid all uniformed police and shake off any attempt to tail him. To establish proof of Fabrizzi's involvement, two plainclothes undercover detectives have been brought in.

Your job is to help them, make a note of the robberies committed [shown as] and follow Fabrizzi's route exactly. You will find that each picture of the city is linked to the next one so it should be easy to keep track of him. By collecting the evidence you will have a cast-iron case against Fabrizzi when you raid his premises at the end.

At the same time you must always know the whereabouts of your two identical detective colleagues. They will either be blending into the scene or working in disguise.

Good luck! Keep a clear head and a sharp lookout and you will soon rid the city of the devious Masterthief.

Solutions at the back of the book will help you if you are truly baffled by his routes!

You must first find Fabrizzi's second-hand store, where you will see that the shelves are empty. Fabrizzi has made his first move. Find him, then trace the route he has taken to see what his first theft is. Your detective colleagues are there on the scene of course, but not easily recognizable!

MANNOX

SPARX

Where did you last see Fabrizzi? Spot the same location here and work out how he gets down into the drain system and crosses the city unseen. He carries out his second burglary en route. What does he steal? What are those detectives up to?

Fabrizzi couldn't possibly have climbed the museum scaffolding without passing in front of the curators at the windows, or could he? What do you think he steals this time, and where are those two colleagues of yours?

The museum is a paradise for the Masterthief - so many corridors to hide in and so many things to steal. What does he choose? He must dodge the curators and open and close the doors very quietly to avoid getting caught. There is also plenty of cover for the detectives!

HOTEL

1
2
3

It is a point of honour with the Masterthief never to give to charity so how does he cross the park without meeting a lady with a red and yellow collection tin? What two things does he take for his shop and what are those detectives up to this time?

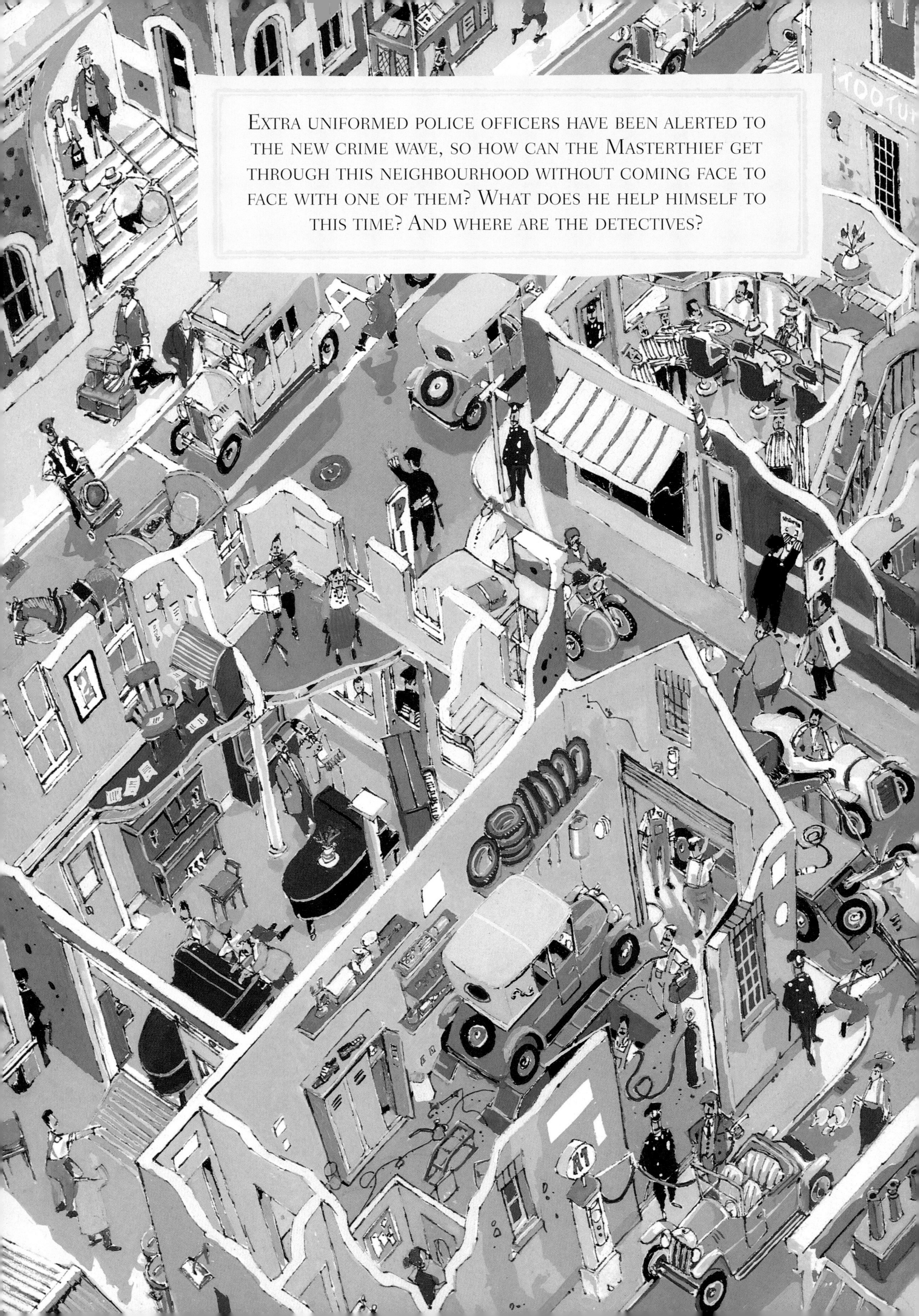

Extra uniformed police officers have been alerted to the new crime wave, so how can the Masterthief get through this neighbourhood without coming face to face with one of them? What does he help himself to this time? And where are the detectives?

SCARAMOUCHE
EINSTEIN

HOT DOG
HOT
5
SNACK
TERMINUS
TERMINUS
TERMINUS

The Masterthief has never paid for a train ticket in his life. With a little luck he can cross the station through the carriages to avoid the police who are looking for fare-dodgers. He is in such a hurry that he only goes through open doors and never closes them again – but he still finds time to steal something!

SINGER
SINGER

It is easy to blend in to the crowds of a busy market, but not so easy to avoid meeting an officer on the lookout for a suspect. How does Fabrizzi make his next theft? And where are your detective friends?

The power station is for Authorized Personnel only, so which way will the Masterthief go to avoid meeting any of the staff? The station offers plenty of good cover for the detectives, but what on earth does the thief steal this time?

Even with his huge sack it is just possible to squeeze between the cars in this massive traffic jam, but how does he get past the traffic cops? He may have to crouch down really low to avoid being seen. What does he steal on the way?

GUNNARSSON.
KENNEDY'S
2

It is the rush hour on the subway, and even the Masterthief has to follow the rules of the escalators. This makes it difficult to avoid uniformed officers. Not only does Fabrizzi manage that but he also robs someone on his way as well. What does he take this time, and can the detectives keep up with him?

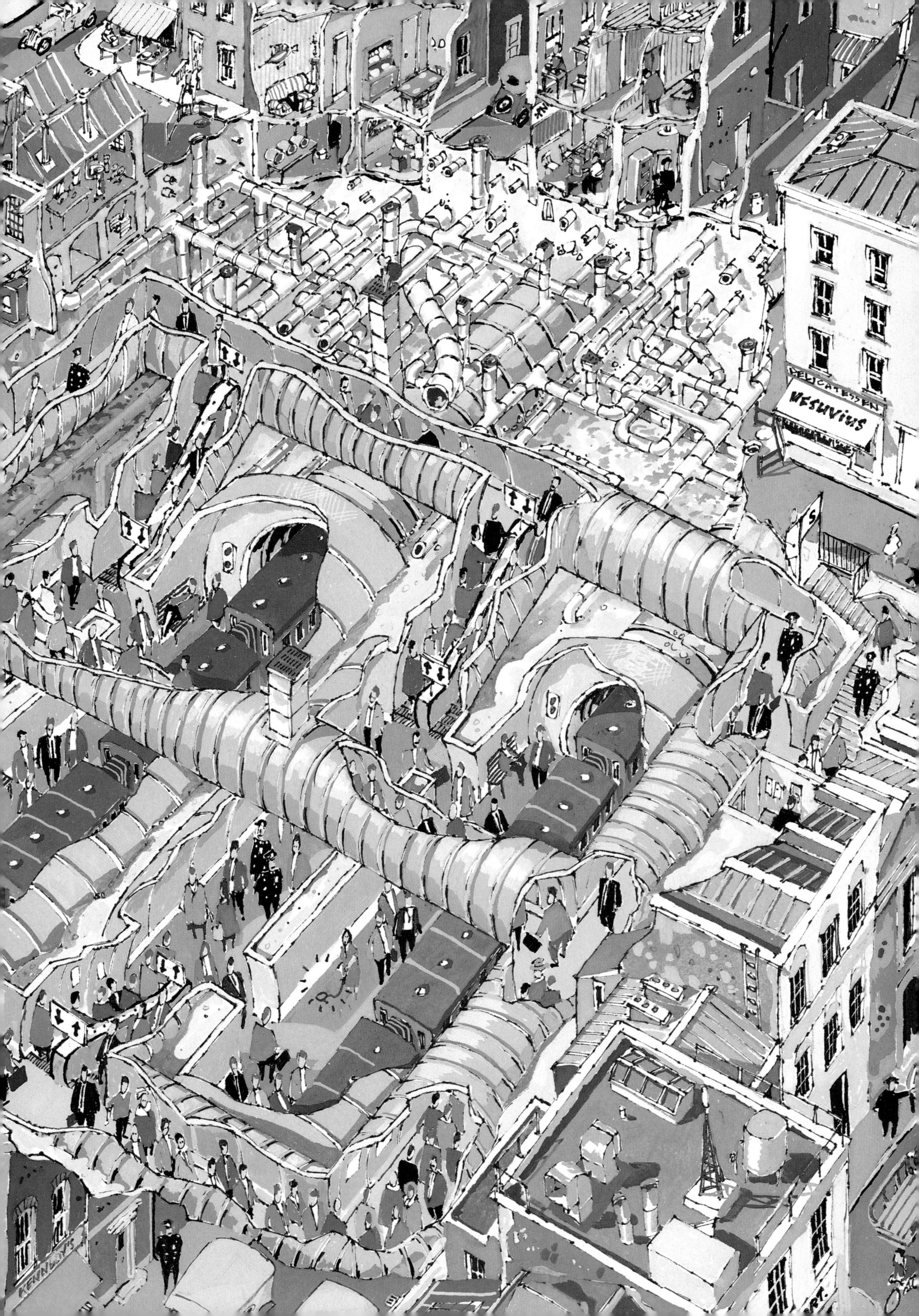
DELICATESSEN
VESUVIUS

ROOMS
ENGLISH SPOKEN
HABLAMOS ESPAÑOL
ON PARLE FRANÇAIS
WIR SPRECHEN DEUTCH
WIJ SPREKEN NEDERLANDS
21
FITZCOHEN
4.99
LO IDON
NEW YORK
PALERMO
PA..IS
2.99

THE EARLY MORNING RAID ON THE FABRIZZI SECOND-HAND STORE WILL BE A FIASCO UNLESS YOU AND YOUR DETECTIVE COMPANIONS CAN MATCH THE GOODS ON DISPLAY WITH THE ROBBERIES COMMITTED THE PREVIOUS AFTERNOON. DO THEY MATCH? IS FABRIZZI THE MASTERTHIEF?

SOLUTIONS

⊕ UNDERCOVER DETECTIVES

⊛ THE CRIME

○ MR FABRIZZI

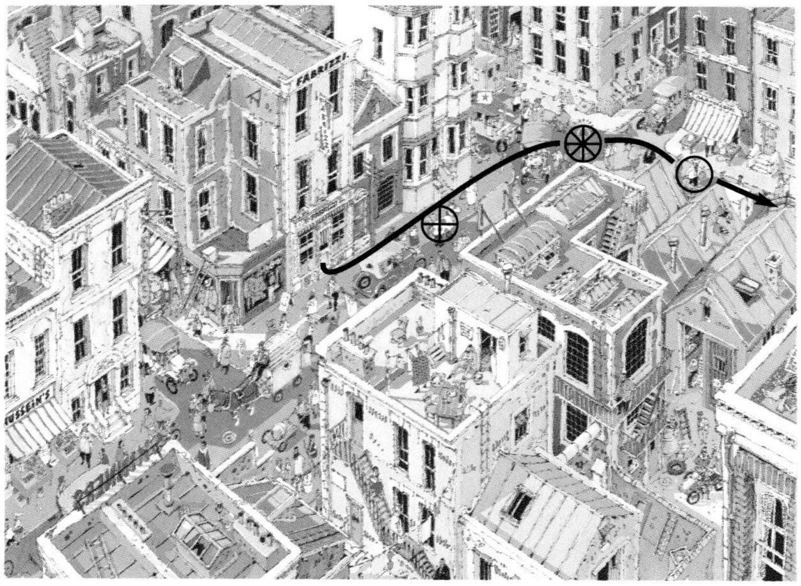

⊛ A HAT

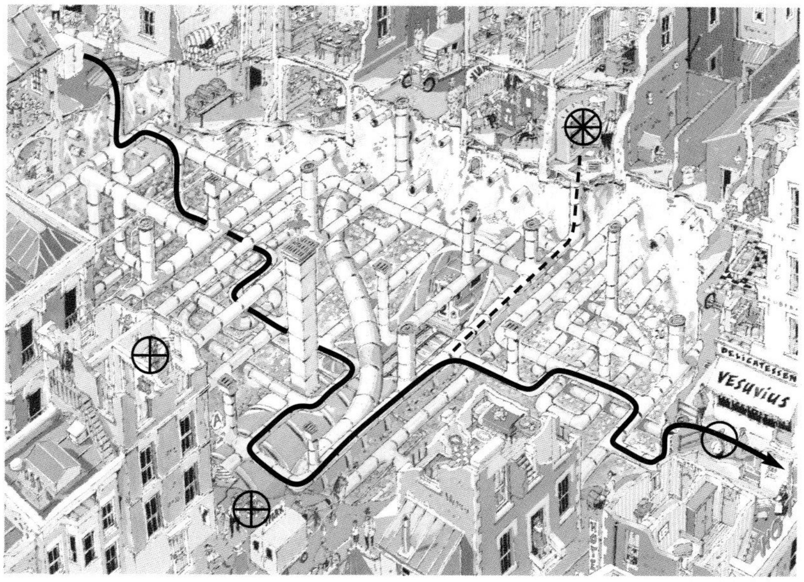

⊛ BAG OF MONEY

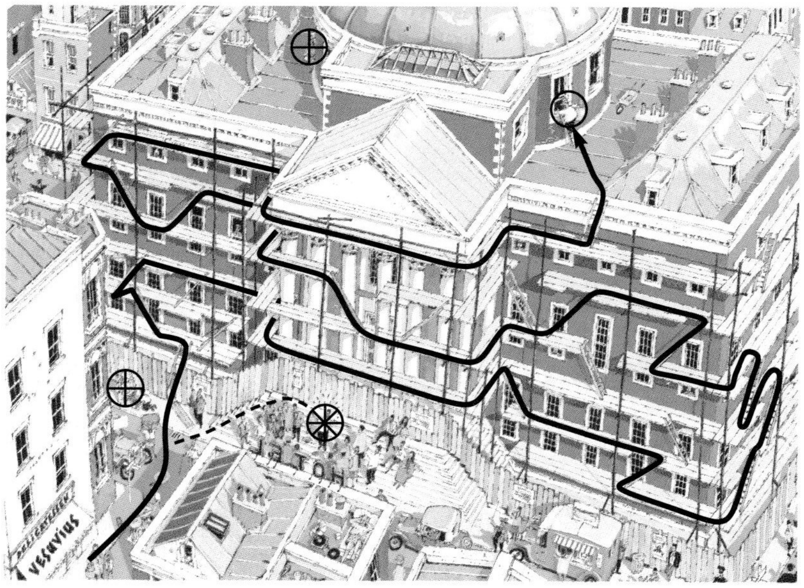

⊛ THREE SKITTLES

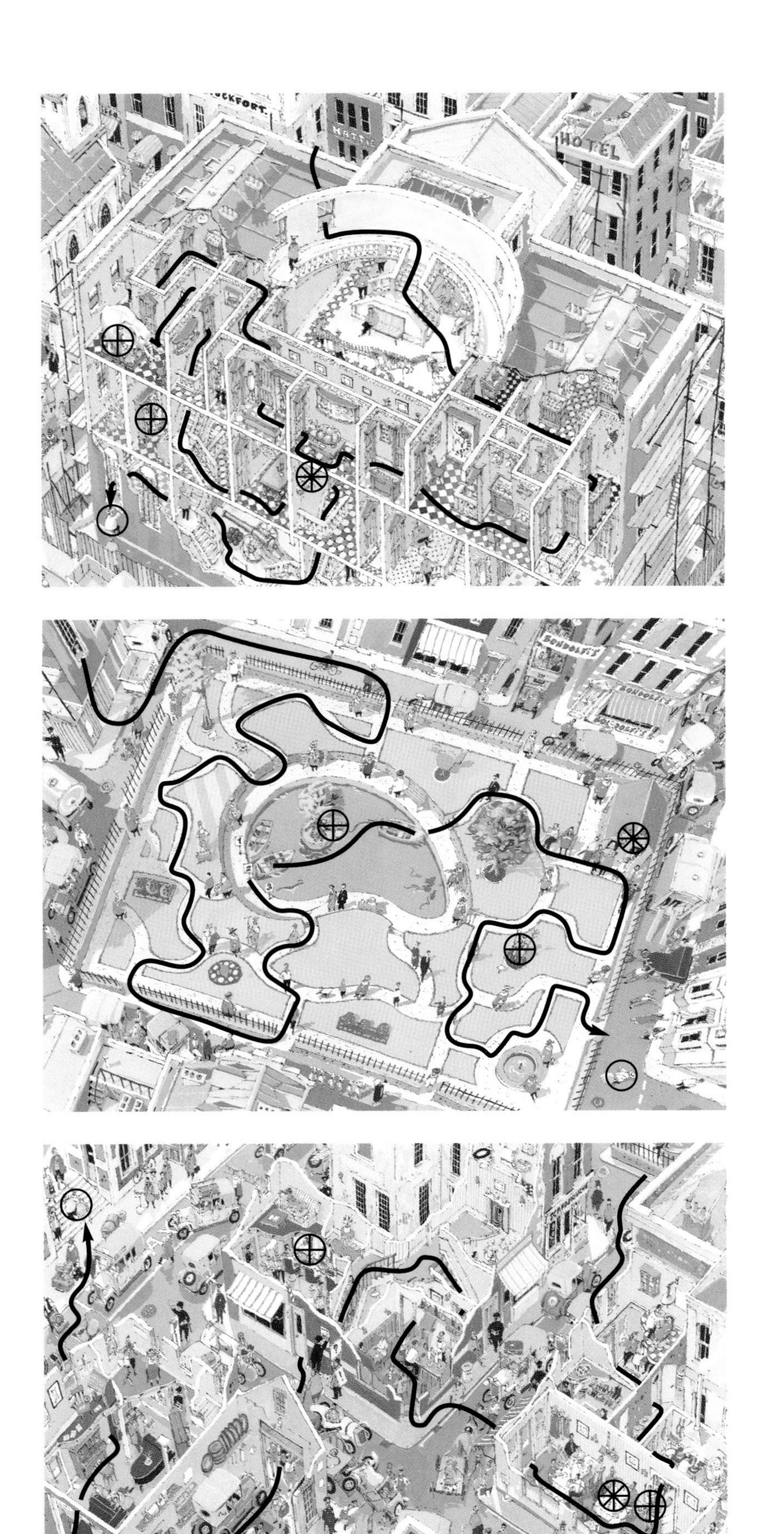

A BUST ⊛

TWO WC SIGNS ⊛

CHAMPAGNE ⊛

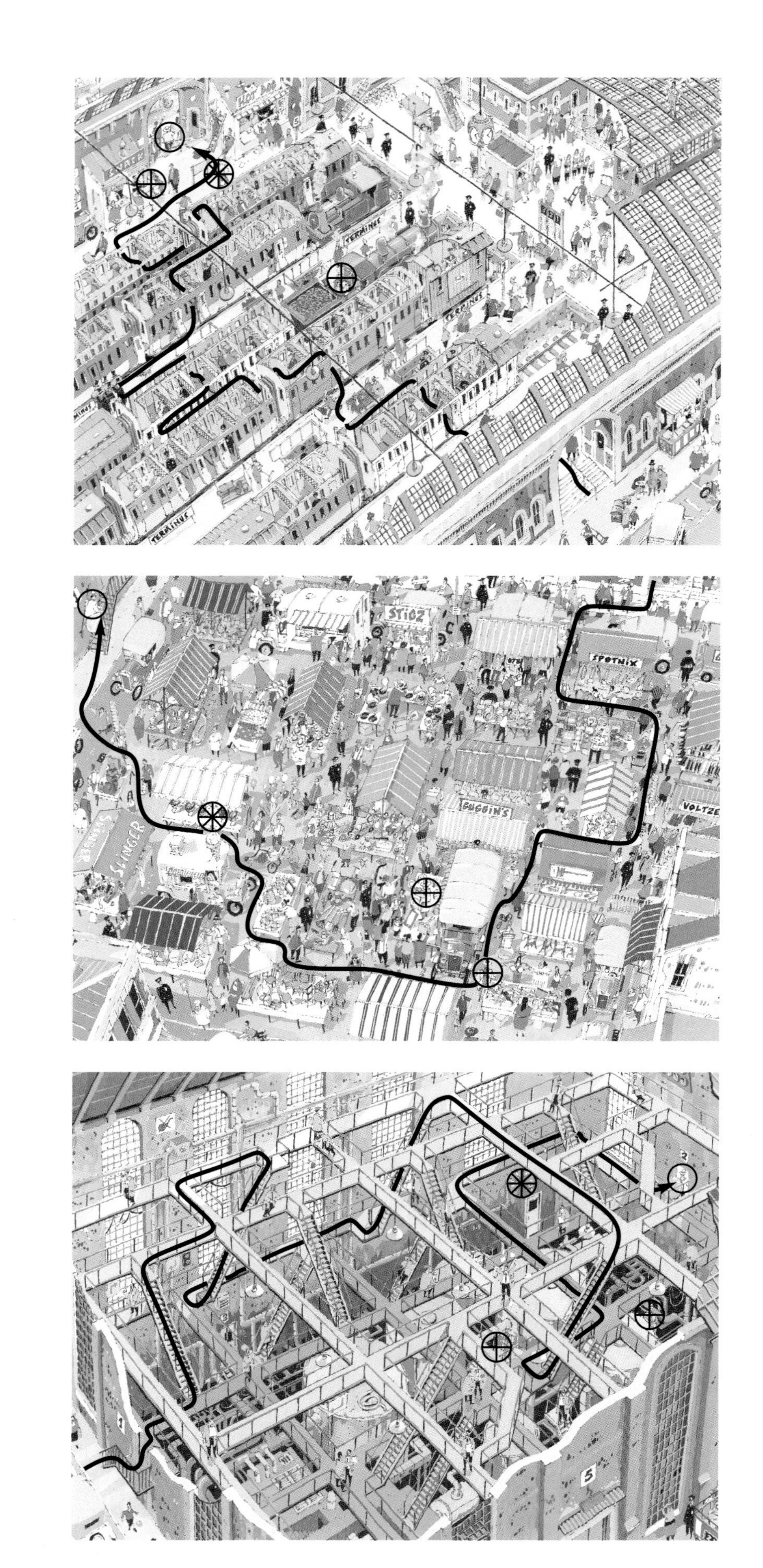

A MAN'S WIG

A LAVATORY

A LAMP

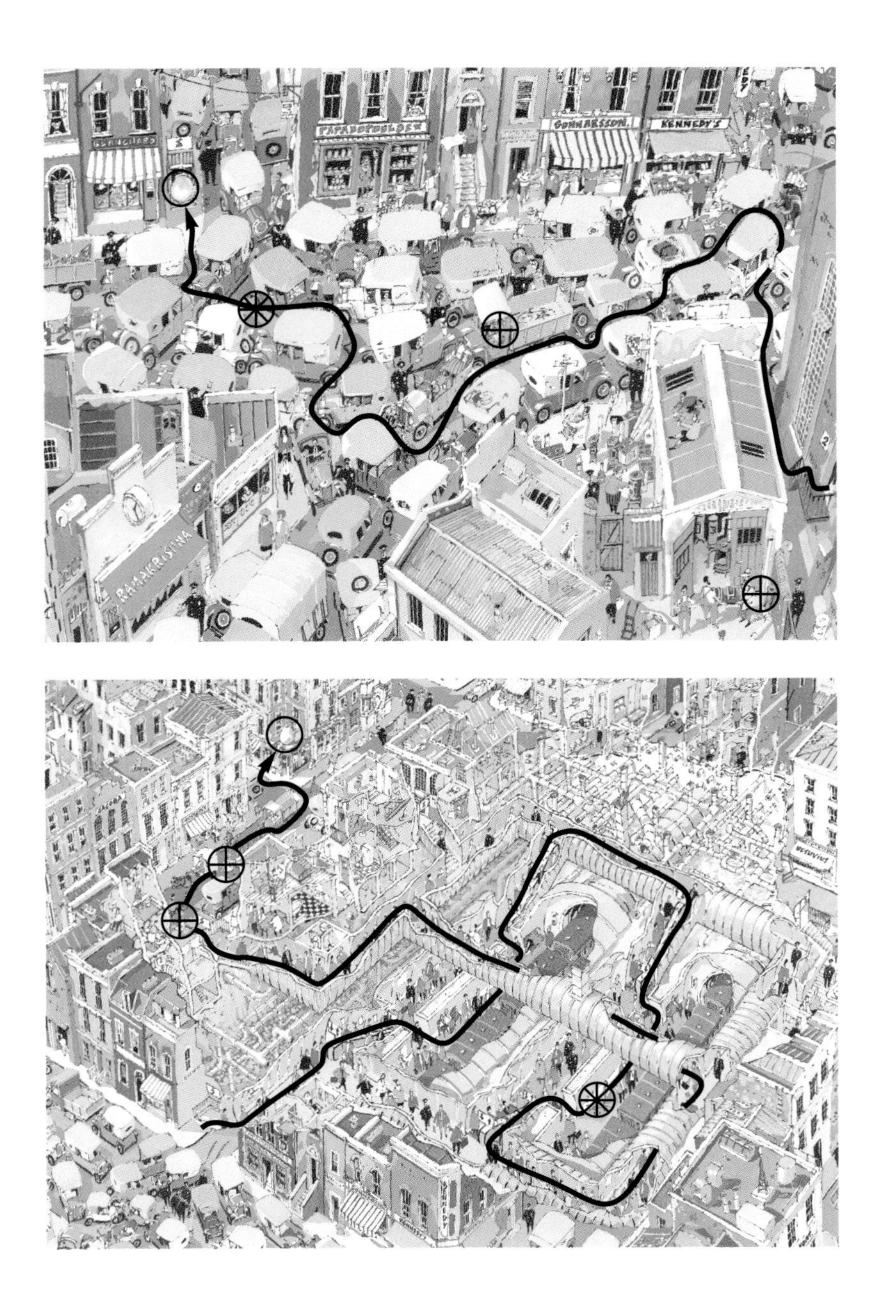

A WHEEL ⊛

A DOG ⊛

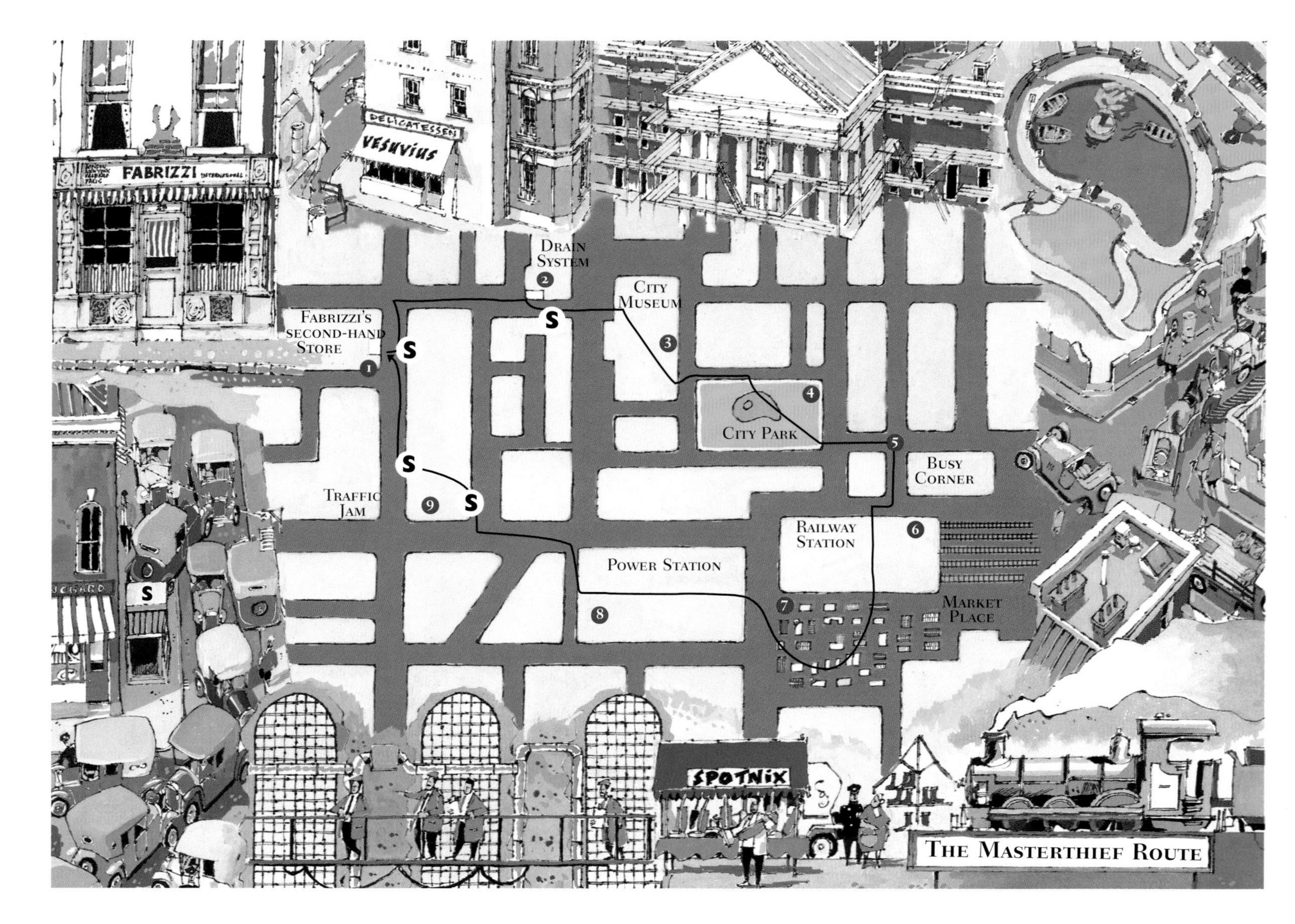

First published 2000
1 3 5 7 9 10 8 6 4 2

First published in the United Kingdom in 2000 by
Jonathan Cape, The Random House Group Limited, 20 Vauxhall Bridge Road
London SWIV 2SA

The Random House Group Limited UK Reg. No 954009

A CIP catalogue record for this book is available
from the British Library

ISBN 0 224 04687 X

Printed in Singapore